by

Sandra Glover

First published
April 06 in Great Britain by

PUBLISHING

© **Sandra Glover 2006**

The moral right of the author has been asserted in accordance with the
Copyright, Designs and Patents Act 1988

ISBN-10 1-904904-86-6
ISBN-13 978-1-904904-86-1

Educational Printing Services Limited
Albion Mill, Water Street, Great Harwood, Blackburn BB6 7QR
Telephone: (01254) 882080   Fax: (01254) 882010
E-mail: enquiries@eprint.co.uk   Website: www.eprint.co.uk

Contents

Chapter 1
MY Terrible Teacher

My best mate, Taz, thinks I've gone mad. Cracked up. He still claims it was all a coincidence. That there was nothing odd about what happened to Mr Barron at all.

"Think about it, Jamie," Taz keeps saying. "Just calm down and think about it. It's not possible, is it?"

Well, maybe not. But the more I go over it, the stranger it all seems . . .

That Wednesday, just before half term, had started normally enough. Badly but perfectly normally.

"Late again, Jamie!" Mr Barron yelled, the minute I set foot in the classroom.

"Sorry," I muttered, trying to squeeze past the large body, which blocked my way.

"Sorry!" he said, pointing at the clock. "Is that all you've got to say?"

"Yes, I mean, no," I stammered, wishing I didn't have to come to school at all.

At least not while Mr Barron was our teacher.

"So, amaze me, Jamie," he sneered. "What's today's excuse?"

"Er, Mum's still in hospital."

"And that means you have to be late for school, does it?" he asked.

"Sort of," I said. "We all have to help out, see? Dad makes breakfast. Jade sorts the little ones out. Gary takes the dog for a walk. I feed the goldfish and the cat."

"Couldn't you feed the goldfish *to* the cat?" Mr Barron said, in a weak effort to be funny. "That might save a bit of time. Or get up earlier?"

"I did!" I told him.

"You fed the goldfish to the cat!" Annie Bell shouted out. "Ugghhh!"

"No!" I said. "I meant I got up early. But after I'd fed the cat, he was sick. He's old and he's got a bad stomach. So I had to clean up the cat mess, mop the floor . . . "

"Stop!" said Mr Barron, pressing his hand on my head, almost crushing my skull. "I only wanted to know why you were late, Jamie. If I'd wanted to know all about sick cats, I'd have been a vet, wouldn't I? But I'm not. I'm a teacher."

"Pity," Taz muttered, as I sat down.

"And teach is what I intend to do," Mr Barron said. "If you're ready!"

We all stared, as he scribbled some numbers on the board. Mr Barron had only joined the school in September but it seemed much, much longer. Up to then we'd been doing all right. Our old teacher said we were lovely but Mr Barron called us stupid, lazy and naughty.

He had a way of getting to you, wearing you down, so the very thought of school made you feel sick. He'd certainly made me feel sick that Wednesday morning . . . so sick that I didn't notice him hovering over me. Not until his fist slammed down, so hard that the whole table shook.

"I just asked you a question, Jamie," he bawled.

"Er . . . did you?" I said.

"Yes," he said. "And it's simple enough, even for you. Now what's bigger . . . three quarters or three eighths?"

"Three . . . er . . . " I was sure I knew the answer. But it wouldn't come. Not with him standing there, yelling all the time.

"Three what, Sunshine?" he snapped.
"Elephants? Daffodils? Spaceships? I
suppose it's all the same to you, isn't it?
Come on, Jamie. We haven't got all day.
Which is bigger?"

"Quarters," Taz hissed, as I stared wildly round the room.

"That's right, Taz," said Mr Barron. "At least someone's not as daft as they look, which is good because I've got some sheets for you to do. More for homework. And, Jamie . . . you can go and sit at my desk. I'd like to see what sort of pig's mess you make of it without Taz to help you."

I picked up my chair, stomped over to Mr Barron's desk and slammed the chair down. Not exactly good behaviour, I know, but I'd completely lost it by then. I hated him. Hated him more than I'd ever hated anyone in my life before.

I still do, I suppose. But after what happened . . . well, I can't help feeling just a little bit sorry for him.

Chapter 2
Plotting Revenge

"Oh, well done, Jamie!" said Mr
Barron, at the end of the lesson. "You've got
two right. Lucky guesses, I expect."

He went on to sneer at some of the
others, even Taz who'd only got one wrong.

"I'm sick of him!" Taz said when we got outside. "We're gonna have to get rid of him."

"Oh yeah," I said. "That'll be real easy, won't it?"

I mean, everyone had tried all the obvious stuff, including my dad. I'd been such a grump over the Christmas holidays that he'd stormed into school on the first day back, demanding to see the Head.

"I've had enough!" he told Mr Low. "That new teacher's no good. Jamie's not learning anything and he's stressed out all the time!"

"Er, I'll have a word with Mr Barron," Mr Low had said.

"A word," Dad had bellowed, "it needs more than a word! That man's got no right being a teacher!"

"He hasn't hit anyone," said Mr Low.

"No," Dad agreed.

"Besides," Mr Low had said, wearily, "how would I find another teacher now term's started? I can't even get enough cleaners, for goodness sake! I'm doing crossing patrol myself because we can't get anyone to do that either. Honestly, I'm worn out!"

He'd looked worn out, too. Completely shattered. In the end, Dad had just apologised and slunk out!

So fat lot of good that was! But at least he'd done better than Taz's mum. When she'd come in to complain, she'd ended up joining the cleaning team! Which was great for Mr Low but it still left us with the worst teacher on earth, didn't it?

Taz just shrugged that Wednesday break when I reminded him.

"Anyway," I said, "it's not so bad for you, Taz. You're clever. But I swear my Maths is getting worse. I don't get fractions at all."

"It's easy,' shouted Taz, above the noise of the traffic. "You just picture it, don't you? Pretend you were chopping up an apple. Halves, quarters, see?

Or, even better, pretend you were chopping

up Mr Barron!"

Taz started chopping and pretending to throw bits of Mr Barron around until he made me laugh. But sadly, my cheerful mood didn't last long. Mr Barron made sure of that, didn't he? At the end of the afternoon, he kept us late, giving out the homework.

"Ah, Jamie," Mr Barron said, holding the very last sheet above my reach. "I take it we can expect you at nine o'clock sharp, tomorrow? With the work?"

"I'll try," I told him. "But . . . "

"I know," he drawled. "Mummy's still in hospital. And we can't cope without our mummy can we? Dare I ask when she might be coming out of hospital?"

"It depends," I told him, "on when the baby's born."

"Baby?" said Mr Barron. "You mean your mother's only having a baby? I thought she was ill or something."

It really got to me that! The way he smiled when he said it. Like it was nothing!

"She is ill," I said, "really ill! It's not going well, this time."

Mr Barron looked a bit shocked. And I thought, for one stupid minute, he was going to say something nice, for a change.

"Mmmm," is what he actually said, "probably comes from having so many kids. How many is it? Nine? Ten?"

"Five," I said, clenching my fist, wanting to punch his big, fat stomach.

"And baby makes six," he said.

"There might not be a baby, you stupid man," I wanted to scream. "She might lose it. She's really poorly!"

But I didn't. I just grabbed the sheet, pushed past Mr Barron and crashed straight into Taz who was waiting outside.

"Did you hear him? Did you hear what he said?" I shouted above the sound of the vacuum cleaner Taz's mother was pushing.

She switched it off when she saw me. "Are you OK?" she asked.

"I'm fine," I lied, not wanting to be held up any longer. "Honest. Got to go."

"You be careful crossing that road," she shouted after me. "Mr Low's already come in. And it's getting dark!"

So I did what she said. I was careful. I stood by the kerb, looking left, right, and left again. Only it didn't make any difference how many times I looked. Cars, vans, motorbikes and buses, were all whizzing past. Headlights full on. Wipers beating back the rain. Totally ignoring the zebra crossing.

Honestly, you could stick a real zebra on that road and cars would still drive straight over it!

I was just thinking I'd be stuck there for ever, when I heard the voice. And that's when the day started to get seriously weird.

Chapter 3
Merry Christmas!

"Want to cross, dearie?" the voice asked.

I swung round and, joy of joys, there behind me was a lollipop lady! Goodness knows why I hadn't spotted her sooner. She wasn't exactly easy to miss with her white coat trailing around her ankles. Not to mention the massive lollipop pole stuck in her hand!

"Merry Christmas," she said, tucking bits of wet, grey hair, underneath the hat, which came down almost over her eyes.

"Sorry?" I said, thinking I'd misheard with the noise of the traffic.

"Merry Christmas," she repeated.

"Er, thanks but it's er, February," I pointed out.

"I know that, dearie!" she said, beaming at me. "I'm just introducing myself. Meredith Christmas. It's my name. But most people just call me Merry."

"Right," I said. "Your parents had a strange sense of humour, did they?"

"Oh no, pet," she said. "It wasn't their fault. Plain Meredith Moon, I was, when I was born. But then I went and married a Mr Christmas, didn't I?"

I wasn't sure Merry Moon was much better than Merry Christmas but I didn't say anything. I didn't get chance!

"Lovely man, was my last hubby," she was muttering. "And I don't mind the name. No, not at all. Lets me bring a bit of Christmas into people's lives all year round, that's what I say."

She giggled as she spoke, which made her sound more like a kid than an elderly lady.

It also made her sound completely mad, which was a bit unnerving.

"Look, I'm late," I told her. "So could I cross now?"

"Oh, yes, sorry," she said. "Only I'll have to be careful. First time I've done this, you see. I've been meaning to come and help out but I've been so busy recently. With my other job," she added.

"What's that then?" I asked, as she made no attempt to get me across the road.

She bent down. Not very far because she wasn't much taller than me anyway.

"I'm a fairy godmother," she whispered. "And this," she added waving the

pole around, "is my magic wand. In disguise,
of course!"

Fantastic! Wonderful! Wasn't that
just my luck? They'd finally got a lollipop
lady and she'd turned out to be a member of
the raving loony society!

"You don't believe me, do you?" she asked, cheerfully.

"Er," I said, backing away in case she turned out to be a dangerous loony rather than the harmless sort she seemed to be.

"It's always the same these days," she said. "Nobody believes anymore."

I looked at her standing there, in the rain, with a massive grin on her face.

"No," I said, "I don't suppose they do!"

"Modern kids," she said. "You're all the same. There's no magic in the world anymore. No sense of fun. All that stuff they teach you these days muddles your heads."

It wasn't *my* head that was muddled, I thought, looking at the traffic, tempted to make a dash for it.

"Plenty of time," said the lollipop lady, putting her hand on my arm, "plenty of time."

"No, there isn't!" I said, trying to make her understand. "I'm late! Mum's ill! I have to get home."

"And you can dearie," she said, "just as soon as you've made your wishes."

"Wishes?" I said.

"Yes," she said. "I told you. I'm a fairy . . ."

"No," I said, totally fed up. "No you're not. No way are you a fairy anything!"

"Oh yes I am, young man!"

"Oh no you're not!"

Irritating as it was, I had to laugh. It was like I'd suddenly found myself living in some crazy pantomime. A wicked 'Barron' back at school and now some nutter claiming to be a fairy godmother!

"Oh yes I am," she said. "I'm a fairy godmother and it's my job to grant wishes. Three wishes are standard in needy cases like yours."

"Look," I said, edging away, right into a huge puddle. "I don't need any wishes. Honestly! I don't even want any. Save them for someone else, eh?"

"Oh, go on!" she said, sidling up to me.
"Give it a go. Make a wish. It can't do any
harm, now can it?"

So there I was, standing in a muddy puddle, on the wrong side of a dark street, in the freezing rain, with a mad lollipop lady who wouldn't let me cross the road until I'd made some wishes! Just how bad could a day get?

I was soon to find out.

Chapter 4
The Accident

As I was wondering how to escape, there was a sudden flash of light in the lollipop lady's dark eyes.

"Go on," she urged. "Make your wishes. But be careful. Be serious!"

"Serious?" I said, as I stepped out of the puddle. "Let me get this right. You tell me you're a fairy godmother called Merry Christmas and you expect me to be serious?"

She looked dead hurt when I said that and I couldn't help feeling a bit sorry for her. It wasn't her fault she was nuts was it? Mum's always telling me you have to be nice to people like that. Not tease them or be mean.

"OK," I said. "I wish I was better at Maths. Will that do?"

"Oh yes," she said, clapping her hands and dropping her lollipop pole. "Very good. This is such fun, isn't it? Much better than crossing a boring, old road!"

Well, no. No, it wasn't, which is why I picked up the pole and headed towards the road. She grabbed the pole off me. She was surprisingly strong for an old lady.

"And such a sensible boy!" she said. "Wishing to be good at Maths. Who'd have thought it, eh? Most lads these days ask to be pop stars or famous footballers."

"Fine," I said, "but now I just wish . . ."

"Careful!" she shrieked. "Careful what you wish for."

Right, I thought. Let's get this over with. Ask for anything, Jamie. Money. A pet dinosaur. Mr Barron's ugly head on a plate. Anything. Anything to get away!

Then I saw that funny light in her eyes again and it stopped me. Yes, I knew it was only a reflection from a street lamp or something. But it seemed to burn right into my brain, telling me to be serious. Crazy, I know, but that's how it felt. And I started to think about the important things. The things I really wanted.

"If this was for real," I found myself saying. "If you were a fairy godmother . . . which you're not . . . what I'd really wish is for my mum to hurry up and come out of hospital."

"Lovely!" she said, waving her lollipop around, accidentally cracking my head.

"Lovely?" I repeated, as the crack made my senses click in again. "My mum's in hospital and you think that's lovely?"

"No pet! I meant it was a lovely wish. And don't you worry! Everything's going to be fine. Your mum will be out soon after her operation and you'll get an extra surprise."

Surprises, I could do without. And as for an operation! What was she on about?

"You're just trying to humour me, aren't you?" she said, sadly. "You don't really believe any of this."

"No, funnily enough I don't," I snapped, as all the anger of the day suddenly exploded. "Mum's not even having an operation. She's having a baby. But it's all going wrong! And the least I can do is go and see her. Or help out at home. But I'm not even doing that, am I? Because Mr Barron kept me late and now I'm wasting time with some stupid old woman who thinks she can wave her magic lollipop pole and make it all better!"

The hurt look returned. Her thin shoulders hunched, folded in on themselves, as if she was shrinking in front of my eyes.

And it reminded me of myself, when Mr Barron was being horrible. And I wanted to stop. I really did. But somehow, I couldn't. Somehow, I just kept shouting in her face.

"But you can't, you mad, old bat! Nobody can. And if you want to live in your crazy fantasy, well that's great. Wonderful. But I just wish you'd stop pestering me and let me cross this road."

Not that I bothered to wait. As I was yelling, I'd spotted a gap in the traffic! Maybe my only chance.

"Stop!" she shouted, as I darted forward. "Watch . . . "

Her voice faded in the sudden blare of car horns, screeching brakes and skidding tyres.

There was a wall of red, a rush of air. A car coming towards me so fast I was sure it was going to slam right into me. But no. I made it to the other side. And it was only when I stood there gasping, shaking, that I realised something was wrong. Very wrong.

The traffic had stopped. There'd been a shunt. Two cars were locked together. And, on the zebra crossing, lay a figure.

A white figure and a broken lollipop pole.

Chapter 5
Deadly Serious

People were getting out of cars, yelling into mobiles. Others were running from the school. I don't know how long it took me to move. It felt like ages before I could unfreeze my limbs, cross the road and kneel beside her.

She wasn't bleeding. Surely that was a good sign? On the other hand there was no colour, no movement. Her eyes were closed. This wasn't pantomime-land any longer. It wasn't irritating, crazy or funny. It was serious. Deadly serious. As I started to cry, Mr Low gently pulled me up.

"The lad ran out," the driver from the red car was saying. "I swerved. I didn't see her following! I must have hit her."

"I saw it too," said Mr Barron. "Stupid boy just ran out!"

"Shut up," I yelled at him. "Shut up!"

"All right, lad," said Mr Low, holding me firmly and staring at the broken pole.

"Who on earth is she? I didn't hire a crossing patrol."

The strangeness of those words barely sank in at the time.

"It's Mrs Christmas," said Taz's mum, bending over her. "And she's breathing, thank goodness."

"Mrs Christmas?" I said. "That's her real name? You know her?"

"Sort of," said Taz's mum. "She moved into the flats a couple of years ago. I met her when she helped out at the greengrocers, when Mr Smith was bad with his back. Remember the Smiths? They sold up and moved to Spain after they won the lottery."

I didn't answer because an ambulance had arrived. Besides, I didn't care about the Smiths or where they'd moved to. All I could think about was poor Mrs Christmas and how it was all my fault. If I hadn't lost my temper. If I hadn't been so mean. If I hadn't darted across the road.

"Come on, Jamie," Mr Low said. "I'll take you home."

"I can't," I said, "I should stay with her."

"I expect that's the last thing she needs," said Mr Barron. "Waking up to find you hovering over her!"

"Don't worry, Jamie," said Taz's mother, putting herself between me and Mr

Barron before I could lash out. "It wasn't your fault, love. It was an accident, that's all. Me and Taz'll go with her. I'm sure she'll be all right."

As Mr Low led me back to the school car park he peeped into the caretaker's shed.

"I thought so," he said, as we got in the car. "The lollipop's gone. And the coat!

She must have taken them. But why?"

"She said she wanted to help out," I told him. "But I don't think . . ."

I paused, trying to choose the right words.

"I don't think she was . . . quite well."

We sort of left it at that. Mr Low seemed more worried about me than anything. Kept asking how I was feeling. Guilty, tired, wet, screwed up! The list was endless. All I wanted to do was curl up and sleep but there was no chance of that.

"Where've you been?" my sister shrieked, as soon as I got home.

"There was an accident," I said, "outside school. Lollipop lady got run over."

No point saying anymore because Jade wasn't listening.

"There's been a change of plan," she said. "Dad's already gone to the hospital. They phoned to say he was needed straight away."

Straight away. That didn't sound good. And Jade was obviously dead worried 'cos she was even more bad tempered than usual.

"I'm going to get Matty and Kate ready for bed. Gary can make us a sandwich. And you can do your homework!" she snapped.

Gary pulled a face at her. He's the eldest. Almost sixteen. But Jade's the bossy one. Usually she drives me nuts but that night I just didn't care. All I wanted was for the phone to ring. For news of Mum. And poor Mrs Christmas.

But the phone stayed worryingly silent.

Chapter 6
Shocks and Surprises

Eventually I got my homework out but it was hopeless.

"Jade!" I shouted. "Come and help me with these fractions."

"I can't," she yelled. "I'm bathing Kate. Ask Gary."

"No use asking me," said Gary. "I'm in Set 5 for Maths, aren't I? Hey, Matty, stop eating the dog's food!"

"Nice," said Matty. "Mine!"

"No, it's not yours," Gary said. "And it's not nice. It's yukky. Come on. Get up and we'll get you a lovely sweetie instead."

"Don't give him sweets," Jade shouted. "I've just done his teeth. Give him a bit of apple."

Apple! Hadn't Taz said that apples might help with the Maths? I grabbed one out of the bowl.

OK. Cut into 2. Then 4.

Slot them back together. Right, so three-quarters must be bigger than a half. Now chop into 8 . . .

"I hope you're going to clear up all this mess!" Jade moaned when she came down.

"Yeah," I said. "I've finished now. Can you check it?"

"Mmm," she said, looking at my book. "It's all right."

"Is that all right, as in OK? Or all right, as in none of them wrong?" I asked.

"None wrong, as far as I can see."

Neat, I thought as I started to clear up. That apple trick really worked! I was still scraping pips off the table when the phone rang, so Jade beat me to it.

"Hi, Dad!" she said. "How's mum? What? She can't have!"

Me and Gary watched as Jade clutched the phone to her ear.

"Yeah. Course. No, you stay. We'll be fine. No, I'll tell them."

She put the phone down, shaking her head.

"What's happened?" I yelled, unable to stand it any longer. "Tell me. Tell me."

"We've got a new brother," Jade said.

"Yesssss!" yelled Gary.

"And," Jade added, "a sister."

"Uh?" said Gary. "You mean they can't tell? Like it's a bit of each or someatt?"

"No, dumbo," said Jade. "Mum's had twins!"

"Twins?" Gary mumbled. "She can't have! She had a scan. There was only one baby!"

"Dad says one was tucked right behind the other," said Jade. "That's why the scan didn't pick it up. And why Mum had to have the operation."

"Operation?" I said.

"You know," Jade said. "Where they cut the tummy open and get the babies out that way."

"Is she all right?" asked Gary. "Is Mum all right?"

"Sure," said Jade. "Dad says she's fine."

I shivered. The thought of Mum being cut open made me feel sick. But it wasn't just that. There was something else. Something niggling in the back of my brain.

An operation? A surprise? Wasn't that what Mrs Christmas had said? The extra baby was certainly a surprise. Not to say a total shock!

It was coincidence though, wasn't it? Just like it was coincidence that I'd got all my Maths right for once. It was nothing to do with magic. Just apples and a bit of common sense. But then the third wish popped into my head.

"I wish you'd stop pestering me and let me cross this road."

And I *had* got across the road. But Mrs Christmas hadn't. So she'd certainly stopped pestering me but in the worst possible way.

Three wishes. And they'd all sort of come true! Freaky, I thought, shuddering. Definitely freaky!

Chapter 7
The Disappearance

It was the stress, of course, making me imagine things. Wishes! Fairy Godmothers! If I wasn't careful I'd end up as mad as Mrs Christmas. Best to stop thinking about it. Do something useful instead. So I rang Taz. No reply. I left a message but Taz still hadn't called when Dad got home.

"Are you all right?" Dad asked, before he'd even taken his coat off. "I bumped into Taz at the hospital. He told me about the accident."

"What accident?" said Jade.

"I told you, Jade! The lollipop lady got run over. Did Taz say how she was, Dad?"

"Yes, she's fine. It was amazing, Taz said. There was hardly a mark on her."

"Oh, that's brill," I said, barely able to believe it.

"Taz reckoned she kept asking about you," Dad said. "Wanted you to know it wasn't your fault."

That was really nice of her! Especially after calling her a mad old bat and everything. It made me feel dead guilty, which is why I got up early next morning and made two cards. One for Mum and one for Mrs Christmas.

I was going to drop them at the hospital but, after doing my other jobs, I was late again so I ran straight to school.

The shouts from the classroom warned me Mr Barron was already in a bad mood. But no. As I got nearer I realised it was the wrong sort of shouting. What the heck was going on in there?

Only one way to find out. I pushed open the door. Everyone was running round shrieking, like they were out in the playground or something. And there was no sign of Mr Barron.

"Where is he?" I asked Taz.

"Dunno. He hasn't turned up yet."

That was strange. Mr Barron was never late. Not ever. He might have been the world's worse teacher but he was always early.

"Anyway, great news about the twins," Taz said. "Weren't expecting that, eh?"

"Er, no," I said, "not exactly. Only it was a bit odd because . . . "

"What?" asked Taz.

Taz is my best mate. Usually I tell him everything. But lollipop ladies disguised as fairy godmothers? Maybe not.

"Nothing," I said. "It doesn't matter. Anyway I got your message about Mrs Christmas. She was definitely OK, was she?"

"Sure," said Taz, "apart from a bit of concussion."

"Concussion? What's that?"

"You know," said Taz, "when you get a bump on the head. It can send you a bit strange for a while. It was quite funny really. Poor thing kept trying to tell me she was a fairy godmother."

"Fairy godmother?"

"Yeah," said Taz. "The doctor says it'll pass in a day or two but it was like she really believed it! She grabbed me when I tried to leave. Absolutely wouldn't let go until I'd made a wish."

"A wish?"

"Have you turned into a parrot or something?" said Taz. "Repeating everything I say!"

"Sorry . . . it's just that . . . I mean, did you?"

"Did I what?"

"Make a wish?"

"Course I did! I had to, didn't I? Or I'd have been there all night."

"Er, what did you wish?" I said, feeling suddenly cold.

"Oh, I just asked if she could turn Mr Barron into a big, fat, juicy worm," said Taz, grinning.

"Er, I'm not sure you should have done that, Taz," I said, looking at Mr Barron's empty chair.

***

"I don't believe I'm doing this," Taz said, as we sneaked out of school. "I'm going to be in right trouble if my dad finds out. Jamie, are you listening to me? This is crazy! Mrs Christmas is not a fairy godmother and she hasn't turned Mr Barron into a worm!"

"So why isn't he in school?"

"He's probably got a cold!" Taz wailed.
"Just because someone takes a day off
school doesn't mean they've turned into a
worm! It's a coincidence, Jamie. Just like
your three wishes!"

Yeah, I know I said I wasn't going to
tell him. But I had to, didn't I? After what
he'd said about Mr Barron.

"So come on," Taz whined. "Let's go
back to school, eh?"

"You go back if you want to," I said,
striding off towards the hospital. "But I'm
going to find her. I have to!"

Chapter 8
Out of this World

"I'm afraid," the nurse said, "that you can't see Mrs Christmas. You're too late."

"Too late?" I muttered, thinking something awful had happened, during the night. "You mean . . . "

"I mean," said the nurse, "that she left this morning. She insisted she wanted to go home."

Taz was tugging my sleeve but I didn't move because I'd spotted a file on the desk, hadn't I? An open file. It's not easy reading upside down but I managed to make out her address. Only Taz was dead set against it.

"No way, Jamie," he said. "No way are we chasing after her. We're going back. Mr Barron's probably turned up by now, so I hope you've got a good excuse about where we've been!"

But Mr Barron hadn't turned up.

"No one's been able to contact him," I told Taz at the end of the day. "Don't you think that's odd?"

"Odd, yes," said Taz, "but it has nothing, repeat nothing, to do with worms or fairy godmothers."

"Yeah," I said, pulling the card I'd made out of my pocket. "You're right. But I may as well go round, give her this and just ask . . ."

Taz groaned but he agreed to go with me. We found the block of flats, took the lift up to the fifth floor and, as we walked towards number 59, the door opened. As if she'd been expecting us!

"Come in," Mrs Christmas said. "Come in."

Instead of moving forward, we both stepped back. I mean, you're not supposed to go into strangers' flats, are you? And Mrs Christmas certainly looked strange. All sort of excited with that light in her eyes again.

"Er, I brought this," I said, handing over the card.

"Lovely dear," she said. "But I'm quite well. Very well. In fact, I'm going home now."

She *was* home, wasn't she? So maybe she imagined she was still in hospital. Maybe she wasn't quite as well as she thought. She grabbed two battered cases from the hall, stepped out into the corridor and closed the door to the flat.

"Er, wait," I said, following her towards the lifts. "There's something I need to ask."

She stopped, put the cases on the floor and looked at us.

"About what you told me yesterday," I said. "I mean you're not really, er, a fairy godmother?"

"No, of course not," she admitted, as Taz smirked. "But you knew that, didn't you?"

I nodded, uncertainly.

"I like to help people," said Mrs Christmas, sadly. "But it just isn't possible these days. Nobody believes in fairies. Smart kids like you start asking questions. Working things out. And if anyone ever finds out that I'm really an alien . . . "

Her hand shot up to her mouth.

"Alien?" shrieked Taz. "So you're telling us you're an alien now? As in, from another planet?"

"Of course I mean from another planet," she said, a bit snappily. "Where else would you expect an alien to be from? Blackpool?"

"Come on, Jamie," Taz whispered, grabbing my arm. "She's nuts."

"No I'm not, young man," she said.
"And, amongst other things, I've got very good hearing."

"Those other things," I said. "Do you mean like granting wishes?"

"Mmm, not wishes, as such," she said, sighing. "But the things you asked for were simple enough."

"OK," I said, as Taz tugged my arm. "The Maths?"

"Easy!" she said, "I just sent some of my own ability into your brain. Just a tiny, tiny bit, of course. Not enough to blow your head off."

"And my mum? The twins? How did you do that?"

"She didn't, you idiot!" screamed Taz.

"He's right," said Mrs Christmas. "I didn't have to do anything at all. I'd seen you and your mum around. I knew she'd need the operation because I'd seen one little baby tucked right behind the other."

"Oh yeah!" said Taz. "You spotted what all the doctors missed, right? With your x-ray eyes, I suppose?"

"That's right, dear," said Mrs Christmas. "Just in the same way I can tell you had pizza and an orange for lunch. Though I'd rather not dwell too much on the contents of your stomach, if you don't mind. The human body still makes me feel quite ill, even after five hundred years of living in one!"

"Five hundred years! Yeah, sure," said Taz.

"The repair job I had to do after that accident!" Mrs Christmas went on. "One little bump and there were broken bones all over the place. Not to mention a kidney squelched to pulp. It was an effort getting it all fixed before the doctor took a look."

"OK," said Taz. "So if you're such a clever alien, how come you had the accident in the first place, eh?"

"I'm afraid," she said, quietly, "that I'm getting on a bit. 807 is quite old, even for a Grooli-ooli. I lost concentration for a moment, that's all. Got Jamie out of the way of the car but forgot to turbo-boost myself."

"Fine," said Taz. "If you say so! Come on, Jamie. Let's go."

"Hang on," I said. "We haven't asked her the important bit yet. About Mr Barron."

"Mr Barron," said Mrs Christmas, thoughtfully. "Ah, yes!"

Chapter 9
Worms and Wishes

"Oh, grow up, Jamie," snapped Taz. "She's not an alien. Surely you don't believe her?"

Did I? Did I believe her?

I don't know. It didn't seem likely that she was an alien, any more than she was a fairy godmother. But I needed to be sure.

I know I hated Mr Barron but I didn't want the poor man to spend the rest of his life as a worm, did I?

"I mean even if she is an alien," shrieked Taz, "even if she did all that other stuff. Turning people into worms is different. It just isn't possible."

"Tricky," said Mrs Christmas, "definitely tricky. But fortunately worms and humans share a lot of the same DNA. Did you know that?"

I didn't even know what DNA was but I'd got the general meaning.

"So you did it? You really did it? I was right! You really turned Mr Barron into a worm?"

"Certainly," she said. "Is there a problem?"

"Of course there's a problem!" I shouted, as Taz pretended to bash his head against the wall. "I mean, I know he's the worst teacher ever. But you can't leave him as a worm. It wouldn't be fair."

"Mmm, I know," said Mrs Christmas. "When I checked on him earlier, he'd already upset a lot of other worms. One poor thing was tied up in knots, trying to strangle itself. Another had thrown itself in front of a blackbird. It's not fair on them at all. So I'd be happy to restore Mr Barron to you . . . if you're sure."

She'd pulled what looked like a calculator out her pocket. In fact, Taz insists it *was* a calculator.

"There," she said, pressing a few buttons. "That should do it. I just need to send the information to the right spot. It won't take a second. Now, is there anything else I can do for you before I leave?"

"No!" said Taz, as Mrs Christmas picked up her cases and stepped into the lift.

I was about to follow but Taz grabbed my arm.

"What did you do that for?" I said.

"No way," said Taz, "are we going into a tiny space with her! She's nuts. You surely don't believe all that rubbish, Jamie. Please tell me you don't!"

"OK, I don't," I shouted, running downstairs. "But you did have pizza and orange for lunch! And there's still some things I need to ask. Come on. We'll catch her at the bottom."

We easily raced the lift down, only when the doors opened the lift was empty!

"Where's she gone?" I said.

"Back to Grooli-whatever-it-was?"
said Taz. "Or maybe she just got off at
another floor. Who cares?"

I cared. But there was no point telling Taz. He wanted to go home but I managed to persuade him to look around first. See if we could find her. But we couldn't. She'd completely disappeared!

By that time even Taz was a bit worried. Not because he believed the alien stuff but because he thought Mrs Christmas was still poorly. He thought she might have wandered off somewhere. Not knowing what she was doing. So he got his mum to check. Ask around a bit.

And, from what she found out, it was all perfectly OK!

Mrs Christmas had been telling people she was planning to move back 'up north'.

Which is possible, I suppose. And just a touch more likely than beaming back to Grooli-ooli!

But then there was the business of Mr Barron, wasn't there?

He came back to school after half term and I was so pleased, I actually managed to smile at him.

He didn't smile back.

He was as grumpy as ever.

Possibly even more than before but in a quieter sort of way. He'd sit, for ages, at his desk, just staring out of the window, trembling whenever a bird flew past!

By Easter, he'd quit. As well as his
sudden fear of birds, Mr Barron had been
having a lot of nightmares, apparently.

About being trapped underground!

And can you believe it? Taz still says it's all coincidence! That lots of teachers suffer from stress these days. Especially ones like Mr Barron who don't really like the job at all. It had nothing to do with Mrs Christmas, Taz says.

Well, I don't know. I only wish I did. But I guess that's one wish that will never come true.

Unless, of course, Mrs Christmas comes back one day.

Also available in the Reluctant Reader Series

PUBLISHING